Bad Wedding

by

Catherine Forde

First published in 2009 in Great Britain by
Barrington Stoke Ltd
18 Walker Street, Edinburgh, EH3 7LP

www.barringtonstoke.co.uk

ISBN: 978-1-84299-615-7

Printed in Great Britain by Bell & Bain Ltd

A Note from the Author

One of the things I love about writing stories is that I can take an event where **nothing** is meant to go wrong – like a wedding. And I can make **everything** go wrong.

I can invent people and make them do terrible things. In the end it's only a story and no one in real life gets hurt.

Making a wedding go wrong was great fun. I know people plan their Big Day for a very long time. They often spend a fortune on the dress, flowers, cars, cake and the party ... I just can't understand it. I think it's such a waste of money. The more perfect and fancy the wedding, the more boring and silly it all is.

I'd rather read about a wedding, even a Bad Wedding, than go to one any day.

I hope some of you will feel the same way ...

To my big boys.
Take heed.

Contents

Chapter 1
A Word of Warning

Are you a big fan of weddings?

Do you want a story about a pretty bride in a stunning frock?

A dashing groom? Maybe in a wee kilt?

Do you want page-boys and flower-girls running about the story? Cute as buttons.

And confetti?

Fancy hats?

Sunshine?

White doves?

A cake that looks and tastes as if angels made it?

Do you want soppy speeches that have all the people at the wedding dabbing away tears of joy and sadness?

And music that gets everyone up dancing? Even the mothers-in-law?

I Do, I Do, I Do, I Do ...

And do you want a hot bridesmaid in this story too?

Well, I'm sorry.

If that's the kind of wedding story you want – oops. I hope you haven't splashed Rice Krispies or dropped jam on this book already. Then you can take it back to the shop. Ask for a refund. Because you won't be reading *any* fluffy stuff in these pages, I promise you.

This is about a *Bad* Wedding.

All thanks to me – the Bad Bridesmaid.

Don't say I didn't warn you.

If you still want a wedding story that's pink and perfect, ask for your money back now. Go and buy *Hello!*

Or *OK.*

Those mags are full of fairy-tale weddings. Proper ones. Where brides look like Jordan. They show up to the church in coaches the shape of pumpkins, for God's sake! And as for their bridesmaids ...

Yes.

Well, in fairy-tale weddings the bridesmaids look like models, don't they? All tarted up in slinky, sexy dresses. In colours that flatter their hair and their skin.

You never see grumpy, ginger-haired bridesmaids in frilly orange charity-shop frocks on the pages of *Hello!*

Hel-lo!

You don't see ginger-haired bridesmaids in silly, frilly orange frocks full stop! Not ever.

What bride wants a bridesmaid who looks like a mega *Solero* ice-lolly anyway?

No bride does.

Unless the bride wants to teach her bridesmaid a lesson she'll never forget.

Chapter 2
Bad Wedding History

I keep trying to tell Lucy that bridesmaids never wear frilly orange dresses. But it's too late.

"Boo hoo," she says.

This is on the afternoon before Lucy's Big Day.

Lucy's the bride-to-be, by the way.

And she's my big sis. Half-sis, really. You'd never know we had the same mum. We don't look one bit like each other. Lucy's old. Twenty-five or something. And we're so different. As different as the Scissor Sisters. Always have been.

Chalk-Cheese.

Night-Day.

Lucy's a smart lawyer. Me? I'm not smart at anything.

And the only reason I'm Lucy's bridesmaid at all is because there's no one else. The two good mates she *really* wanted went off and got themselves pregnant. Right after Lucy set the date for her wedding.

Bad planning there, eh?

The first mate told Lucy, "I can't waddle up behind you in a big posh dress looking like a pig in silk!"

The second mate, who's going to be very, very pregnant on the wedding day, was scared her waters might break – *sploosh!!* – while

Lucy was saying "I do." (That would be such a blast!)

So Lucy was stuck for a bridesmaid. She needed someone. *Anyone.*

She had to find a late sub.

Guess who?

A few weeks ago, out of the blue, I got this phone call.

"Hiya, Jane, it's Lucy," the person on the phone said.

"Lucy who?" I answered.

"Lucy your big *sister*, silly," Lucy said in a tight little voice. She sounded a bit hurt that I didn't know it was her. I knew fine well, of course. But I just L.O.V.E. winding Lucy up, bad half-sis that I am. Down the line I heard Lucy suck in a big gulp of air. She sounded like she was going to dive into a deep dirty pool of muck. Very fast she spat out, "Look, you know how me and Cuth are getting married soon?"

"Uh?" I grunted.

So what? I was thinking. *And how can you marry a bloke with such a stupid name? Cuth. How can anyone be called Cuth, for goodness' sakes?*

"Jane, are you still there?" Lucy's voice turned snappy when I didn't answer her. She's like that. Nippy. "Did you hear me? *Will* you be my bridesmaid? Please?"

Tee hee. Begging me to be her bridesmaid must have *killed* Lucy.

We've NEVER got on. Lucy's neat and tidy and smart. Just like her surname – Smart. My surname's Drain, by the way. When Mum married my dad, Lucy kept her real dad's surname. No wonder. Smart's a much better surname than Drain, isn't it? So Lucy's Smart

and I'm Jane Drain. And we're half-sisters.
Different dads. Same mum.

Anyway, Lucy's a goody-goody. Prim.
Proper. I'm not one bit like that.

Before Lucy moved to London and found her
Mr Right – her Cuth – oh, man, did I drive her
crazy!

I'd borrow her clothes. Then put them back
dirty and smoky and sweaty.

Steal her make-up.

Use up all the credit on her mobile.

I'd squish my big feet into all her fancy
high shoes. I'd wear them to college to show
my pals how daft they looked on me. Or I'd go
clubbing in them. Put them back in their boxes
with heels missing and straps broken.

The only things I never nicked from Lucy
were her boyfriends. Well, they were all

boring plonkers. With ugly beards. Lucy's into beards. Big, bushy beards. Creepy, yeah?

And I never nicked Lucy's music. But I did *hide* her CDs a lot. Just so I wouldn't have to listen to the soppy singers she likes. Or have to listen to her singing along with Katie Melua, Celine Dion (ugh!), Mariah Carey (ugh! ugh!). And that James Blunt guy. His CD went in a skip ...

Oh, Lucy loved me for that!

That's a joke, by the way. Me and Lucy have so much bad history.

She HATED my guts when she lived at home. I know, because she told me. All the time.

And nothing's changed.

"I *really* hate your guts, Jane," Lucy's saying all over again.

And she's been saying it non-stop since she came home for her stupid wedding.

Chapter 3

Back to that Orange Dress

So. Now you know a bit more about us – the bride-to-be and her Bad Bridesmaid – it's time to go back to what was happening on the afternoon before the Big Day.

Heeeee-re's Lucy!

She storms into my bedroom. She rips open my curtains. She doesn't seem to care that I'm under the covers and I'm begging her, "No. My head. Please. Keep them shut." Lucy just rips open those curtains.

I told you she still hated my guts.

"There!" Lucy chucks a black bin-bag at me. "Wear *that* tomorrow."

"Wear what?"

I'm sitting up in bed. Before I can open my eyes to look in the bin-bag, I have to pat around for my sunglasses. Lucky they're handy. I put them on quick. Ooooh! *The light hurts*, I'm thinking. Then I pull this dress Lucy's got me out of the bin-bag. And – oooh! Oooh! Oooooooya! – it gives me a massive shock.

And it's not just an electric shock, from all the sparky static in the cheap, scratchy fabric. It's the blooming colour of the dress! It's so bright, my eyes hurt even more.

"You can't make me wear this!" I gasp. "It's like a glow-stick."

"You'll have to wear it. Too late to get anything *nicer*," Lucy snaps back at me. "Serves you right."

"Ugh! It's *orange*. Nylon. With puffy sleeves. And it's a size 18! I'm not a whale."

"You're no size 10 either, are you, honey-pie?" Lucy hisses back.

Miaow. Cheeky cow!

Lucy was looking at herself in the mirror. Smoothing her hands over her bony hips.

"You're lucky to have a dress at all," she says. "I only had time to nip into that Oxfam shop next to the beauty salon. Then I went to visit poor Cuth. He's only just starting to wake up," Lucy goes on. "I'm getting married tomorrow. Remember? You're meant to be looking after me. *You're* meant to make sure me and Cuth have a perfect day. Instead of –"

Lucy's voice is so high and angry, I have to put my hands over my ears.

"You bought *this* in that charity shop?" I ask.

I need to change the subject. Move away from any stuff about Lucy and Cuth. Talking about the groom-to-be just now is *not* helping Lucy's nerves.

I sniff the dress. There are dodgy stains down the front of it.

"Ugh." The armpits of the dress smell dodgy too. They pong of stale sweat. Oh, dear. I make a quick dive for the bucket next to my bed. Just in case I puke.

Again.

That *would* be bad news.

You see, I hoped my tummy was settling down at last. I haven't eaten a thing for three days, after all. Nothing. Not since I noshed every dish in an all-you-can-eat curry buffet. That was for a bet. Seemed like great fun at the time.

And it was.

The best fun I ever had.

But let me tell you, eating a tramp's belly-button cheese would seem like fun after Lucy's Hen Night. What a yawn-a-minute *that* was. Well, the first few hours were yawn-a-minute. While Lucy had her little 'cocktail party'.

Of course, a little cocktail party was NOT my idea of a Hen Night in the first place.

Chapter 4

The Hen Weekend *I* Wanted

If I'd had my way, me and Lucy and her mates would have gone to Blackpool. We'd have had the hen-weekend of our lives. Then Lucy wouldn't be yelling at me on the day before her wedding. She wouldn't make me wear the ugliest dress in the world. Cuth, her groom-to-be, wouldn't be in such a bad way that no one knows if he'll even get to the church ...

And yes, yes. I *am* coming to that.

But first I'll tell you about the Hen Night I wanted. The Hen Night I sorted for Lucy. In

Blackpool – Las Vegas of the North. I booked a Bed and Breakfast (only £9.99 per person – bargain). And I mapped out the pub crawl I'd take Lucy on. Then I found this pole-dancing club where we'd boogie the night away when the pubs shut. I even rang college to say I was sick. Told my tutor I had the "Blackpool flu". That way I'd have a good few days to dry out when I came back home.

But oh, dear, did the fur fly when I told Lucy what my plans were!

"Blackpool?"

She was so, SO cross. Raging mad with me.

"What sort of slapper do you think I am? I hate your guts, Jane." She went on. And on.

The thing is, I was only trying to be a good bridesmaid. I'd read about what to do in a glossy *Wedding Bells* mag I'd nicked from the dentists. Inside, it said –

18

Top Tips to Make YOU the Perfect Bridesmaid.

Number 1 tip was:

Take the heat off the bride-to-be.

Surprise her with a Hen Night to remember.

Do something she'd never think of doing herself.

Hey, no problemo, I'd thought. I knew what Lucy would *never* think of doing herself – she'd never pole-dance in Blackpool ...

Well, she'd never pole-dance *anywhere.*

Or get smashed off her face.

Or walk up to blokes she'd never seen before and ask for a kiss.

Sorted! I thought. Blackpool, here we come!

As an extra treat, I even booked a stretch limo to drive Lucy and her hen party all the way there.

"Surprise!" I told Lucy when I turned up at her flat in London out of the blue. I'd come all the way down to London on the bus. It was a Friday night. This was about a month ago. You see, that was **Top Tip Number 2** in my mag –

Leave plenty of time between the Hen Night and the Big Day.

No one wants a sore head on their special day!

"Pack a bag," I told Lucy as I threw her this pink satin bomber jacket I'd bought off eBay.

"You're goin' on your Hen Night," I sang as I shoved a glittery cowboy hat on Lucy's head. *"Time to let your hair down."*

"What?" Lucy had a green face-pack on. It cracked like an egg-shell whacked with a spoon. "I'm having an early night," she said. "I'm going to watch the news, then go to bed."

"No, you're not," I told Lucy. "There's a limo outside. So wash your face and phone your mates. Tell them the Pink Ladies are off to Blackpool for a night on the town!"

"Pink Ladies?" Lucy pulled off her cowboy hat and shooed me away with it. When I tried to pin a flashing "Last Chance to Snog Me" badge to her chest, she scowled so crossly that a big chunk of her face-pack fell on to my hand.

But I didn't give up.

"The Pink Ladies are the girls. Y'know? From *Grease*. *'You're the one that I want. Oo, Oo, Oo'*," I sang. I was trying to be helpful.

"Greece?" Lucy looked at me as if I was talking blooming Greek.

"*Grease* the movie – Frenchy and Rizzo and Sandy and John Travolta ..."

I nodded at Lucy but she just shook her head blankly.

You are SO un-street, I nearly yelled into her prissy green face. But I didn't want a cat-fight. So I counted to ten instead.

"Come on. The limo's waiting. There's bubbly in it. We can all get wasted. It'll be mad," I said. I forced a grin onto my own face. A cheery one. *Oh, my God!* I was thinking. *This poor Cuth bloke she's marrying must be a saint!*

Lucy shook her head some more. All the cracks and broken-off bits on her face made her look like a creepy baddie from *Doctor Who*.

"Get drunk and go to Blackpool?" she said. "I can't think of *anything* worse, Jane. Go away and grow up!" Her voice sounded more evil than a creepy baddie from *Doctor Who*. She chucked the pink bomber jacket back at me. Closed the door.

"But the limo," I shouted through her letter-box. "I've only paid the deposit. We'll all need to chip in –"

So there was the Hen Night that never was.

If we'd had that Hen Night, I wouldn't be in all the mess I'm in now.

Pity.

I had to thump on Lucy's door till she lent me the money for the limo. The driver was going to call the cops if I didn't pay up. He was so pissed off about missing the run to Blackpool, he wouldn't even drop me at the bus station. Or give me back the crate of bubbly I'd bought to get the party started. I had to walk three miles across London. In the rain. In my cowboy hat and my pink bomber jacket.

They're back on eBay, in case you're interested.

Chapter 5
The Bad Hen Night

I didn't even think Lucy was going to bother with a Hen Night at all. She never said anything about having one when she came up from London last week and moved back home. She just said she needed 'lots and lots of time to chill out' before her Big Day. I wonder if she read about that in my *Wedding Bells* mag. It said,

All brides-to-be need to find time to relax.

Lucy did that all right. The first few days she was home, she just lay on the sofa, asking

Mum to bring her cups of tea and Kit-Kats. But then, three nights ago – that's just four days before the wedding – she phoned me up from some posh cocktail bar near here.

"Hi, Jane, I know it's short notice," Lucy said. "I'm out with some friends from work who've come up to be here for me on my big day. Pop along if you like. But the bar's pretty smart and dressy. No jeans. And we're just having a cocktail or two – nothing too loud or mad or over-the-top. Not really your scene. And you don't know these girls I'm with. And we really don't want anything wild," Lucy warned.

In other words –

"Please don't bother coming, Jane."

But I went.

Duh!

Too right.

I wanted to rattle Lucy's cage. And have some free drinks.

For a laugh, I dolled up in my slinky blue bridesmaid's dress. Why not? It was the smartest and newest thing in my wardrobe, after all. Lucy had got it for me in London and she'd given it to me when she got home.

"Dressy bar," Lucy had said. "No jeans."

I jazzed up my glad-rags with my mum's mother-of-the-bride hat.

Mum thinks it's "Just fab, fab, fab!" I think it looks like a little red kiddy bucket you'd take to the beach to make sandcastles with. If you ask me, wedding hats are ALL daft. What a waste of dosh! Why do people wear them?

Anyway, I took the hat without asking. Just for a laugh. Along with Lucy's wedding shoes.

But that wasn't *just* for a laugh. Or *just* to piss Lucy off. I mainly wore the shoes to do Lucy a mega-favour.

You see, when I'd been flicking through my *Wedding Bells* mag again, I'd spotted a photo of a bride. She was putting a sticking plaster on her heel. Making a face that said "Ouch!"

DO make sure you break in your wedding shoes before The Big Day.

It said under the picture –

No bride wants blisters on her tootsies.

Oh, dear, I'd thought when I spotted Lucy's wedding shoes on top of Mum's wardrobe. They were next to the daft hat. Still in their box. Not once had I seen them on Lucy's feet. So that's why I wore them to the cocktail bar.

After a night on my size seven feet, Lucy's size five shoes won't pinch anywhere, I told myself as I limped into the cocktail bar. *They'll feel as comfy as old slippers.*

Plus I'll have a giggle. It's not every day a bit of scruff like me wears white satin wedding heels.

27

God knows, I needed *something* to giggle about.

Lucy's Hen Night was so DULL, I don't know why I'd bothered to tart up. I'm not kidding, I could have had a wilder party down the local graveyard with the stiffs. Or talking to my handbag.

Not one of Lucy's pals spoke to me. From the minute she told them, "Oh, everyone. *This* is my half-sister Jane," they bunched up together and froze me out.

Over their soda and limes they talked work talk that had me nodding off.

Then they talked pushing-out-babies talk. I thought I was going to barf up my dinner.

Then they had a big debate about Lucy's First Dance with Cuth. *What should they dance to?* This is what they came up with, for God's sake:

1. "Everything I Do, I Do It For You". (Blugh!)

2. "Three Times a Lady". (Blugh! Blugh!!)

or

3. That song from the film of *Titanic* – "*Near, far ...*"

I couldn't bear to think about it. I'd rather hear someone scratch a fork up and down a window than that Celine Dion dame singing.

To keep myself awake, I kept nipping to the bar in Lucy's high heels. Getting more drinks in for the Hen Night gals. I put them all on Lucy's tab, of course. *And*, of course, I necked a few extra cocktails while I was waiting for all their soda and limes. Come on!

a. *I needed something to take away the pain in my feet.* My poor toes were folded over in Lucy's tiny satin shoes and – ouch – did they HURT!!!

and

b. it *was* a Hen Party.

Some chick had to let her hair down. And I'd never drunk cocktails before. They looked so yummy I wanted to try them all. So I did.

The last thing I remember clearly about the cocktail bar was tossing back a "Wild Thing" (that's vodka, rum, ginger ale and mint). Then I got up onto the bar counter.

"Ho!" I shouted. "See that woman over there? Look, you can just see her behind that fat woman in the flowery smock. Well, the skinny one in the baggy jumper with the cat on the front's my sister and she's getting married!" I yelled at the top of my voice. I stamped on the bar in Lucy's high-heeled bride's shoes till everyone quit sipping cocktails and looked up to frown at me.

"Three cheers for the bride-to-be!" I shouted. "Raise your glasses, everyone!"

"Hey! Stand up, Lucy! Don't be shy," I yelled even louder. "Come on now, Lucy! Wave, Lucy! There she is – 'the bride-to-be'!"

And before anyone in the in the bar went back to their drinks, I gave them all a bit of a song.

You see, this cocktail bar was so blooming dull and boring. And this was meant to be a party! I thought a sing-song might cheer things up a bit.

So I burst into "All I Could Do Was Cry". It's my karaoke song, a golden oldie by Etta James. Funnily enough, it's a wedding song. But not a "ding-dong, here comes the bride" one. It's a blues number – about a girl with a broken heart. She's seeing the love of her life getting wed to someone else. So it's sad. But it's also a million times better than that "Everything I Do, I Do it For You" lovey-dovey moosh. Well, *I* think so.

I still don't know what made me sing it to Lucy. It just popped into my head. Seemed like a good idea at the time ...

Anyway, I'd only sung a little bit of it when Lucy was up at the bar. And not because she wanted another cocktail. Oh, no. She was tugging so hard at the hem of my long blue bridesmaid's dress that I felt the seam rip.

"Shut up, Jane," she hissed. "You're making a total fool of yourself. And of ME. I *hate* your guts, you stupid drunk ..."

So I stopped singing.

Not only because Lucy told me to. I stopped because this bloke next to her started to help Lucy drag me down off the bar. He had a policeman's uniform on.

"Hey! Now we're talking!" I shouted.

I thought this bloke was part of Lucy's Hen Night. That's why I tried to tug his trousers down. "Do a Full Monty!" I was yelling.

32

Silly me! I should have known Lucy's mates are far too boring to book her a strip-o-gram. But that's who I thought the policeman was. Booked to spice up the Hen Night. I did have five 'Wild Thing' cocktails going to my head, after all. And I think that's why I shouted, "Get 'em off! Get 'em off!" till the bloke in uniform warned me I'd have to go down to the police station with him if I didn't pipe down. Oh, dear, I know I'm bad, but I'd *never* have groped his bum if I'd known he was a real cop.

Lucy had to do some *heavy* lawyer talking so I didn't have to spend a night in the cells. She was RAGING with me.

To make everything worse, there seemed to be a small problem with Lucy's wedding shoes ... in fact, there seemed to be a *big* problem with Lucy's wedding shoes. One had a broken strap and the other had a snapped heel. Now, *she* thinks what happened to those wedding shoes was my fault. But I blame that cop. If he'd just let me finish singing, I'd never have

33

done a runner. But he warned me, "Right. You're down the station," so I jumped off the bar.

Snap, went the heel of Lucy's shoe.

Rip, went the hem of my silky blue bridesmaid's dress.

"Out! The lot of you," boomed the boss of the cocktail bar.

And that was the end of the Hen Night part of Lucy's Hen Night.

There were two big holes in my blue bridesmaid's dress by the time I got myself up off the pavement. My knees must have ripped the dress when I went tripping out of the cocktail bar in my broken heel. And there were two big bouncers standing over me. They had their arms folded and they were giving me evils. So were all Lucy's pals. They kept muttering and hissing at me while Lucy tugged her wedding shoes off my feet and scooped mum's wedding hat out of a puddle.

"You always make a mess of everything, Jane," Lucy shouted as she whacked me with mum's hat. "I *really* hate your guts. And look what you've done to my shoes. How dare you steal them ..." she screamed at me like a vixen with her tail on fire.

Then she and her pals stormed off. To their cocoa and their beds, I bet. They left me barefoot in the rain. My fancy blue dress dragged in all the puddles. Blood from my knees was running down my shins.

I must have looked a right sorry state.

Chapter 6
When the Hen Met the Stags

Yes, I must have looked a right sorry state. But when I limped round a corner, I heard someone wolf-whistle at me.

"Wa-hay!" a bloke shouted.

"There's one!" said his mate.

"She'll do," another guy said.

There were about five blokes. They were all wearing daft hats – *nearly* as daft as my mum's red wedding bucket hat. They were standing in front of this other bloke. He was tied up to a lamp-post with that blue and white stuff cops use round a place where there's been an accident. All the blokes were shooting the taped-up guy with silly string.

But when they saw me coming in my tatty dress, they stopped shooting to give me the once-over. The way they were looking me up and down and grinning and nodding, you'd think I was Kate Moss.

It was a wet night, and I was the only female about, and from the state of these lads I knew they were looking at me through beer goggles. Blokes'll wolf-whistle a she-elephant if they've had a few lagers.

Still, after putting up with two hours of Lucy and chums, it felt like things were looking up. I was glad to meet *anyone* who was pleased to see me. Even a few drunks. I gave these blokes a thumbs-up as I walked past. Then the tallest one waved me over.

"Quick. Before you go," he started to say.

He was wearing a wedding veil over his face. "Give this man the kiss of life," he went on. "Poor guy's getting hitched in a few days. Take pity on him."

"Kiss!"

"Kiss!"

"Kiss!"

The rest of the guys all started to chant. They turned their silly string cans on me. I got covered in the stuff.

"Kiss!"

"Kiss!"

"Kiss!"

Duh! Like I was going to snog someone I'd never even seen before. Someone with a baby bonnet on his head! And a beard. I might have been tipsy, but I'm always choosy. And I'm not stupid.

So I made sure I kept a few feet away from them all. I wasn't huffy or snooty. I put my hand under my chin and blew the tied-up guy a kiss.

"Good luck, baby," I told him, with a wink. "You'll need it," I added. I was thinking of Lucy. Nag, nag, nagging poor Cuth. *God help this bloke if his wife is half as bad as her,*" I said under my breath as I started to walk up the street. These guys seemed OK but I wasn't taking any chances.

"Aw," groaned the guy in the veil. "Don't run away. We won't bite!"

"Boo!" moaned the others.

"Leave her alone," I heard the tied-up guy tell them all. Then he called over to me, "Sorry. No harm meant. Just having a laugh."

I kept walking.

"No worries," I called back.

"Might be the last laugh I get," he added. He started to cry like a baby. That's what made me stop. Made me giggle.

I turned round.

I moved closer to the street-lamp.

I lifted my hand to blow the tied-up guy another kiss.

That was when he gave this huge roar. He started fighting to try and get free.

"Jane!" he yelled. "What the hell are you doing out here at this time of night?"

Chapter 7

Bert

"Do I know you?" I asked. I ripped off all the silly string that hung down my face like dreadlocks.

"Jane? *Jane!*" the guy shouted again.

He sounded like Tarzan now. But he looked more like the Hulk when he just ripped out of all the police tape that held him to the lamp-post. He pulled the bonnet off his head.

"It's me! Bert," he said.

"Bert?" I didn't understand.

I shook my head. I'd only ever known one Bert. Years ago. He didn't look like *this* tubby bloke who had a brown shag-pile rug all over his face, that was for sure.

But then the tubby bloke did a little dance in front of me – "Jane. Look. It's me!" he said.

That was when I knew he *was* my Bert all right.

You know that dance where you hold your nose and wiggle down with your knees together?

My Bert and I did it whenever we met each other, instead of saying hello.

"Bert!" I said.

"What are you doing here?" I asked.

And what's happened to you? I thought. But I didn't say that.

The last time we met was about four or five years ago. I was still at school and Bert was *buff*. All his hair was on his head then, not growing out of his chubby cheeks. Back then, I'd had a bit of a secret teenage crush on Bert. OK, he was way too old and way, way out of bounds, but even so ... Bert helped out in this Youth Club I went to. I hung about there like a bad smell. Every night. To get away from the house. Away from Lucy. Bert used to stop me at the door if he saw me walking in with a face on. He'd do his funny dance at me till I cracked a smile. I had to do the dance back to him to prove I'd cheered up.

Bert was a good guy. Kind. He listened to me. Never gave me a hard time.

When he went south to university, I chucked the Youth Club.

Wasn't the same without him.

I was down in the dumps for ages.

And I never thought I'd see Bert in my life again.

Chapter 8
One of the Lads

But here Bert was, back in my life and 100 per cent for real. He was calling his friends over. Making them shake my hand.

"Guys, this is Jane. She's an old mate," Bert told his new mates. Then he told me who they were –

"This is Paul." That was the guy in a fireman's hat.

"And Toby." Toby had a baldy-man wig.

"And this is Max." He'd a crash helmet on top of a long, blonde wig.

"These three guys are up with me from London. It's my Stag Night," Bert said. Then he nodded at the last guy to shake my hand.

"And you know this guy, Jane. He's one from the old days."

The bloke who had called me over to kiss Bert was shaking my hand.

"I'm Gary," he smiled. Then he threw back his wedding veil. "I'm Bert's baby brother. Remember me now? From the Youth Club?"

Phwoar! How would I not remember you? I nearly blurted out loud. Had to bite my lip hard. Gary was tall. Dark. Handsome. Best of all, there was a wicked twinkle in his eyes.

"Gary?" I said his name out loud. I thought if I said his name loud it'd help me remember.

In my head I was thinking hard. Tricky to do when your brain's swimming in cocktails!

The only Gary I knew at the Youth Club had so many spots that me and the other girls called him Jelly Tot behind his back ...

And to his face. I did that when I was in one of my mean moods.

That's because Jelly Tot Gary followed me about non-stop. Annoying me.

"D'you want some chocolate, Jane?" he'd say.

"D'you want a game of pool, Jane?" he'd ask.

"Have you heard of this band, Jane?" he'd want to know. "I think you'd like them."

Back then I just wished Gary'd leave me alone so I could chat to Bert.

How times change!

Now it was Bert who was busy trying to chat to ME but all I wanted was time alone with Gary. Poor Bert. I felt a bit sorry for him. He looked a bit of a saddo now, with his comb-over hairdo. And that beard. It was one of those ones bits of egg would get lost in forever. And his beer belly was so big he looked as pregnant as Lucy's mate. It swelled over the top of his trousers. And all the buttons on his shirt looked ready to pop.

"Gary's my best man next Monday," Bert was telling me. "He's got to get me to the church on time. I'll be in trouble if I don't." Bert slapped his brother on the back.

He didn't see Gary look at me or hear him mutter, "He'll be in trouble anyway. Poor bloke wants to marry the Bride from Hell."

I liked Gary. He looked like one BAAAAD Best Man.

"Yup, I'm getting married, Jane," Bert told me proudly. And just before I could chip in, *How weird is that? I'm going to be a bridesmaid at a wedding on Monday ...* he went on talking –

47

"I'm marrying a lovely, *lovely* girl. And do you know a funny thing? She's from round here. But we met in London. We work together. We're in the same law firm. She's a few years older than you –" Bert's eyes had gone all gooey as he spoke about this lovely girl of his.

"Lucy," Bert said. He was grinning and licking his lips as if the name Lucy tasted of chocolate-covered moonlight.

Lucy? I gulped. I did not have a sweet taste in my mouth. *Lucy the lawyer who lives in London now? Surely not ...*

I started to open my mouth to ask a few questions – *is Lucy's surname Smart by any chance? Does she have a half-sister? And a brown jumper with a cat on the front?* – when Gary gave me a nudge.

"Jane, you used to moan about a Lucy, didn't you?" he said. "What a nippy sweetie she sounded. Too good to be true. You said she hated your guts. She gave you a right hard time," Gary grinned. Then he took the words I wanted to say right out of my mouth. He said them for me.

"Hey. What are the chances of ..." Gary was pointing from me to Bert "... y'know, the chances of Jane's Lucy being your Lucy? Eh, *Cuth?*" he said. He stroked the top of his brother's head – where poor Bert had gone a bit baldy. Then Gary gave Bert loads of little kisses. "What do you think, Cuth-y? What are the chances of Jane's Lucy being your Lucy-woosy?"

"Zero," Bert tutted. It was as if Gary had just said something only a stupid younger brother would ever think of.

"What do you think, Jane?" Bert turned to me. "Zero chance of your Lucy being my Lucy, I bet," Bert turned to me. He was looking for help.

But I couldn't help him. I was too busy thinking about the name Gary had just called his big brother.

Cuth?

I just stared at Bert.

I thought my eyes were going to pop out my head and land on the pavement.

"Cuth?" I asked.

When my voice *did* come out at last, it was a squeak. *YOU'RE Lucy's husband-to-be, you poor, poor man*, I was thinking. Gary must have thought the look on my face had something to do with the name he'd just called his brother.

"Cuth. Stupid bloody name, innit? Sad, man," he said with a grin. "But not as stupid as *Cuthbert*. Did Bert never tell you his real name? It's Cuthbert, isn't it, *Cuth-bert?*" Gary snorted. He was teasing Bert the way I used to tease Lucy.

Only Lucy always fought back.

Poor Bert didn't. He was too sweet. He just patted his beer belly and tried to change the subject.

"Guys, are we going for this curry or not?" He looked round at his other mates.

They just jabbed their fingers at him.

"Cuth-bert."

"Cuth-bert."

"Cuth-bert," they were all saying to each other. Then they started to dance round in a circle and pull silly faces to match the silly name.

I shook my head. *You are Lucy's Cuth. You must be!* I needed to say to Bert, but I was so shocked I couldn't say a word.

"Cuthbert's Lucy doesn't think Bert's a good name for a lawyer. So she's made him change his name to Cuth. And made him grow this."

Gary tugged his big brother's beard. He was winking at me.

"Cuth's Lucy loves telling people what to do. Hey, d'you think your Lucy could be Jane's sister, Cuth? That would be so funny." Gary laughed.

"I don't think so." Bert looked upset. "Anyway, Lucy's never said a word about having a sister," Bert sniffed at Gary. He tried to change the subject again. "Can we get on with my Stag Night now? I'm meant to be having fun." He patted his big belly. "And food is my idea of fun."

"Too right!" I agreed with Bert.

Poor guy.

There was something hen-pecked about him already. Or Lucy-pecked.

"You go and enjoy yourself. Make the most of your freedom," I told him. "It's been lovely seeing you again." This time I gave him a proper kiss on his cheek.

And I think Bert was just happy to have someone who wasn't laughing at him, because the next minute he asked me to join him and his mates.

"Hey, Jane, I know it's meant to be really bad luck to let a girl on a Stag Night," he said, "but if you fancy a bite ..."

What could I say? I didn't want to be rude. So, "Yes," I said. "I'll jolly along with the Stags," I said. "Why not?"

But, oh, dear, if only I hadn't. How different the ending of this bad wedding story would be!

Bert was right – a girl on a Stag Night *is* unlucky.

If only I'd just taken myself off home like a good little bridesmaid ...

But I didn't.

53

"It's great to have you along, Jane," Bert told me as I walked arm-in-arm with him and Gary to the curry house. "You're just like one of the lads."

Oh, my God, if Lucy could have seen us!

"One of the lads? Oooh, I don't know about that, Bert," Gary said. He looked at me just like he used to look at me in the old days, when him and his spots followed me around the Youth Club. This time it didn't annoy me at all.

In fact I was wishing I hadn't wasted so much time blooming running away from Jelly Tot Gary. We sat next to each other at the curry house and we didn't shut up. We had SO much in common now. Like the music we loved, for example. And the music we hated.

"'Everything I Do, I Do it For You'. No way!"

When I told Gary about the crap songs Lucy wanted her and Cuth to dance to, he had to push his chicken tikka away.

54

"Need to do something about that," he said with a groan.

By this time he knew that *my* Lucy was *Bert's* Lucy. Gary laughed so much about it that lager came out his nose and soaked into his naan bread. He said that was the maddest bit of news he'd heard since Bert showed him a picture of this dame in a brown jumper with a cat on the front, and with a big long nose and thin lips and said he was getting married to her.

"We better not tell Bert you're Lucy's sister yet," Gary whispered to me. "He'd send you home. That would be a real shame, Jane."

Gary's twinkly eyes twinkled into mine.

And that's why Lucy's crap Hen Party turned into the best night of my life.

Chapter 9
The Best Night of My Life

Oh, yes. Lucy's Hen Party turned out to be the best night of my life.

So far.

And not just because Bert's Bad Best Man and little old me hit it off like fish and chips.

Another reason the night was brill was that, by the time the curry house shut, I was fifty quid up.

I was the winner of the Stag Night "Who Can Stuff The Most Curry Down Your Gob" competition. I should really have let Bert win.

Gary told me much later that Bert had been in training to come first. He was gutted I beat him. Gary also told me it was spooky that Bert lost. Until this Stag Night curry competition, Bert had never been out-eaten by any *bloke*, let alone a girl.

Poor Bert.

Yes, I should have let him win. Not just because I felt sorry for him; after all, Bert was about to spend the rest of his life with grim Lucy. I'd have to eat all day long to cheer myself up if that was me!

If I'd let Bert win, I wouldn't have had to scoff so much curry and naan and rice and lager myself. I mean I was Out of Order. Noshing up so much on top of all those cocktails I drank earlier.

I'm STILL paying the price three days later. Here I am – stuck in my bed. My head's thumping as if someone's stamping up and down inside it. My belly's heaving. I'll *never* eat too much again. And I will never, NEVER mix my drinks. In fact, I will NEVER touch lager or vodka or gin or rum or whisky or wine again. I have learned a lesson I will never forget.

But three nights ago, with fifty quid up for grabs, and all the Stag blokes chanting, "More! More! More!" at me, I ate and drank Bert under the table.

REALLY under the table.

And now I'm getting closer to the REAL bad part of this bad wedding story.

One minute Bert was cramming a big lump of naan into his gob. Shoving it down with the palm of his hand, bits of it all sticking to his beard. The next he was sliding off his chair.

Bang!

His chin clonked the table on the way down. Then his head banged it too. The poor guy knocked himself out cold.

Max and Toby had to get down on their knees under the table and give Bert mouth-to-mouth. There was blood too – Bert bit a hole into his own lip. And he needed an ambulance. But I heard all about that later.

From Lucy.

At the moment when poor Bert was slipping under the table, I didn't know what was happening to him. That's because Gary and Paul were jogging me round the curry house on their shoulders. On my head I was wearing the last dish I'd just licked clean. I was waving my fifty quid.

"I am the champion!" I remember singing, before all that jogging got too much for my insides.

"Put me down. Quick!" I retched. "I'm going to be ..."

That was when the Best Night of My Life came to an end.

Things have NOT been so good since then ...

Chapter 10
The Truth

Gary had to carry me home on his back like a sack of potatoes. And as he came up the garden path, he met Lucy running down it. Gary told me later that he nearly dropped me. Lucy was in her nightie and curlers and face cream.

"Cuth's in A&E!" she screamed at him. Then she went round the back of Gary so she could scream into my face too. "I might have known you had something to do with this, Jane. Cuth is out cold. I hate your guts!"

Lucky for me I was out cold too. I was drooling and moaning. Lucky too that a taxi was already at the gate. It was waiting to rush Lucy to hospital. She only hung about long enough to give Gary the kind of grief she likes to save for me.

"And *some* Best Man!" she lashed out. "Why weren't you looking after my Cuth? Keeping him away from trouble? He needs stitches, Max said. Three days before my wedding! You and Jane make a right pair ..."

Seeing Lucy freak out before she'd even got to Bert's bedside, Gary did the noble thing. He handed me over to Mum. She didn't know what I'd done to her daft hat yet, so she only gave me a bit of grief for coming home in a state. Then Gary took a brave pill and went off to the hospital with Lucy.

The Bride-to-Be and the Best Man turned up just in time to see Cuth/Bert getting his beard shaved off so the nurses could stitch his chin up. Gary sent me a text to say Lucy looped the loop when she saw her husband-to-be's face.

Not because it was split open and gushing blood and bruised and bashed.

No. She was mad because her Cuth had been hiding three big fat chins under his mug rug.

Everyone, Lucy ranted, would see them in the wedding photos now.

"So – that's just perfect! Thank you, Jane, so much, for ruining my life!" Lucy burst into my bedroom and screeched the moment she came back from the hospital. I was still hanging over my bucket. I'd been doing that for hours. I just wanted to die.

And that's it. That's why this is a Bad Wedding story so far.

Now you know how and why I trashed my blue silk bridesmaid's dress. You know why Lucy can make me wear an ugly orange Oxfam shop dress to her wedding instead. And you know why she can keep marching up and down by my bed growling, "I hate your guts, Jane," while I'm still feeling yuck.

Even if Lucy's groom-to-be *hadn't* ended up in hospital, I've been a crap bridesmaid. Twelve hours before the wedding, I should be running about. Helping the bride.

"You should be helping the bride with a zillion things!" Lucy is screeching now as she stands over me with the orange dress. Flaps it in my face.

"You should be ringing the hairdresser. Making sure my flowers are coming. And that my dress is ironed. Plus you're meant to be keeping me *calm*. But oh, no, you have to go and wreck the most important day of my *life*!"

Lucy's voice is getting louder and louder, higher and higher. She sounds like a seagull fighting a cat.

"You go out and rip the dress I bought you," Lucy yowls. "Then you sick up all over it. It cost me *two hundred pounds*!"

"Sorry. I've said sorry," I mutter. *A million times.* But Lucy is way past listening by now.

"*And* you wear my wedding shoes out on the town," she screeches. "They cost even more than your blue dress!"

Lucy's voice is nearly out of human hearing range. All the local dogs must be putting their paws over their ears and begging for mercy.

She's a blushing bride, that's for sure! Her face is as red as Mum's daft hat. As red as the hat was *before* it fell in the puddle. That's what Lucy is screeching about now.

"You dunked that lovely hat I picked for Mum in mud. It's all out of shape," she yells.

"Yeah, but the mud brushed off," I say.

I'm starting to talk to Lucy in a sing-song voice. Like how the actors on *ER* talk when they want to stop a nutter jumping off a building.

"And there's no problem with your shoes now," I go on.

I point to Lucy's feet and try to smile at her. But Lucy kicks at my sick bucket with the white satin shoes she's been breaking in all day. What's her problem? Two seconds on Google and she found the exact same pair as the ones I busted. But only half the price. They came in the post this morning. I was even able to pay Lucy fifty quid towards the cost of them.

"All these little things are sorted, Lucy. You should be worrying about Bert ... I mean Cuth. His head injury. Gary says he doesn't know where he is yet," I tell her. Inside, I'm praying Lucy scrams. Just for half an hour. Then I can have one last nap. *If I have one last tiny nap*, I think, *I might find the energy for these bridesmaid chores ...*

Of course, as soon as Lucy sees my eyelids droop, she whips the duvet off me.

"Get up!" she yells.

Lucy's voice has got so high and so loud it hurts my teeth. "And try this on so I know it's not too small." She yanks the orange dress over my head.

"Lucy, please let me nip out? Try to buy something else? Something blue. I'll be quick," I beg when I peek in the mirror and see what I look like in the ugly orange frock.

Ugly, I look.

The dress is like a grubby life-jacket with a few old net curtains stitched around the bottom.

It's nearly the same colour as my hair.

"If you make me wear this," I sniff, "I'm going to spoil all your wedding pictures –"

"Oh, you won't, Jane," Lucy rasps. "Because you're not going to be in any of my photos." Her mouth is twisted into a cruel smile.

"But now I've got you up on your feet, you can get cracking on the things I need you to do. Start by ironing *my* dress. I'm going for a bath. Chop chop."

Chapter 11

The Really Bad Part of the Bad Wedding

Get ready.

We're coming to the *really* bad part of this bad wedding story.

It's a few hours later.

But Lucy's still in the bath.

God knows what she's doing in there. Is she shedding her skin? Shaving the palms of her hands? Turning herself into a princess bride?

All I know is that I'm standing in the kitchen, ironing her wedding dress and she's driving me NUTS!

She keeps making all these *private* noises. Sighs. Groans. Ugh! I try not to listen, try not to imagine what she looks like while she's making the sounds. When you haven't eaten anything for three days you can't cope with that gross stuff.

But you know what it's like when you try to shut something out?

Sounds you don't want to hear, or think about, seem to grow louder. They wind you up even more. So, as if Lucy has loudspeakers set up in the bathroom, I'm forced to pick up every splash and snip and scrape and buzz she makes. Oh, and then there's the 'singing'.

While Lucy's groans and sighs and lathers and shaves herself, she tortures me by playing a whole CD. *Every Cheesy Song Jane Hates*, it could be called. No one would buy it, though. Here are some of the tracks:

"Lady In Red".

"Love Is All Around".

"I Can't Smile Without You".

"Flying Without Wings".

"Everything I Do, I Do It For You" (of course!).

... and that bloody *Titanic* song ...

There are other songs, but I'd need another lie down if I gave you the titles. Cliff's in there. James Blunt ... pass the sick bucket!

Anyway, to make things worse, Lucy "sings" along. *"I feel it in my fingers, I feel it in my toes ..."* Her high voice tweets out like an old biddy singing a hymn.

I feel it in my teeth.

But, like a trusty bridesmaid, I keep sweeping the iron over Lucy's wedding dress. Back and forth. That's harder than it sounds. Lucy's voice drives me crazy. So crazy that I nearly drop the iron on Lucy's skirt so I can put my hands over my ears. I can't think straight. Lucy's doing a duet with Whitney Houston now. Their voices are drilling into my head like pick-axes.

"And I ay I y. Will Always Love YOOOOOW ..."

"Shut up," I grit my teeth. I make myself picture Lucy in the wedding dress I'm ironing.

Walking down the aisle.

Walking down the church to meet Bert at the altar.

Here comes the bride, all dressed in white...

I try to picture the pair of them, bride and groom, turning to each other.

They smile into each other's eyes – *I do*.

But do you know what?

This sounds *really* weird. But this is the *really* bad wedding part of this story. I just can't picture Lucy and Bert getting married tomorrow.

No matter how I try.

And yes, yes, I know what some of you are thinking. *Jane can't picture Bert with Lucy because* **she** *wants to be the bride. She's like the girl in that song Jane sang in the cocktail bar. Jealous and broken-hearted because the bloke she loves is marrying the wrong dame ...*

Well, *if* that's what you're thinking, shame on you!

I don't want to marry Bert. Beard? Belly? Old? With hands that have been all over my sister – get real!

I don't want to marry *anyone* right now. I've some fun to have me first! Anyway, me and Bert were mates. I told you that already. Nothing more. And if he's happy with Lucy, then I'm happy for him.

Happy for Lucy too ... I suppose.

Yes.

If the pair of them are meant to be.

But *that's* the problem.

That's what's so weird.

Even when I shut my eyes, and squeeze them tight, and try to make Lucy walk up to Bert and say "I do", *I can't.*

There's just a big black space inside my head.

No bride and groom standing there like a tiny plastic couple on top of a wedding cake.

It's not happening! I close my eyes tighter. I'm trying to picture my sister with Bert again.

"But it's just not happening." I hear my voice. It's a soft whisper. I can hardly hear it over the power-lungs of Lucy and Celine Dion singing together in the bathroom –

"Near, far. Where-ever yoo ..."

Do you know what?

This is the one time in my life when I feel truly sorry for my big sister. Here I am, holding an iron over her wedding dress. I'm listening to her howling out love songs while she shaves her legs for her new husband ...

And I just get this bad, *bad* feeling about her wedding. It's creeping over me.

Even before the doorbell rings.

Even before the letter-box flaps.

And a fist bangs the front door.

Yes, I have this bad feeling about Jane's wedding even before Gary's voice shouts out "Lucy? Jane? I've good news and bad news ..."

I'll tell you Gary's good news first –

Bert was on the mend. Wide awake. Out of hospital.

The bad news ...

Well, bad news for Lucy.

Bert had lost his short-term memory. That clonk to his head in the curry house knocked it out of him.

He'd no idea how or why he ended up in hospital with 20 stitches in his face.

When Gary told him it was something that happened on his Stag Night, Bert said, "Stag Night? Are you about to get *married*, then, Gary?"

Then Bert asked Gary to help him find his razor.

"There's nothing like a good close shave," Bert told his brother.

When Gary told Bert how much his bride-to-be had loved his big bushy beard, Bert laughed so hard he split the stitches in his chin.

"Bride-to-be? Get out of here," Bert told Gary.

And Gary did as he was told.

He came here. Popped over to give Lucy the bad news.

Tell her the wedding would need to be called off.

Well, you can't marry someone who doesn't know you, can you?

That's what Bert told Lucy, too, when she dashed over to throw herself in his arms. "But Cuth, it's me. Your bride-to-be!" she cooed.

"Sorry, I don't know you. And my name's Bert, not Cuth. *Cuth?*" Bert shook his head at the sound of the name. Then he smiled his big, cheery Bert smile. Winked at Lucy. "But I'm happy to get to know you, Lucy Smart," he told her.

Must have had a bit of brain damage!

Chapter 12
Ahhh ...

So this is my bad wedding story, but it can still have a happy ending.

Just because there wasn't a proper *wedding* doesn't mean there was no *party*. All the guests were in town, after all. It was too late to cancel the reception. The band ...

Or the honeymoon. It was all booked and paid for, so Bert told Lucy they might as well go on it. It would be a good chance for him to get to know her better.

Everyone says Lucy and Bert's wedding was the best wedding that never was.

No boring speeches.

No daft hats.

No bridesmaids in ugly orange frocks. That horror Lucy bought me is shoved back in its bin bag. I'll be dropping it off at Oxfam along with a wedding dress. Unworn. Slightly scorched on the skirt …

And so this is the happy ending … *MY* happy ending.

With no bride and groom for the first dance, the bridesmaid and the best man took to the floor. Me in my comfy jeans, Gary in the veil he wore on Bert's Stag Night.

Guess what song I picked? No, it wasn't that bloody *Titanic* tune. It was Etta James, of course.

And I got to be in all of Lucy's "wedding" photos, after all. Me and the hot best man.

"Hey, if I get married for real, it better be as much fun as this," Gary whispered in my ear while we were dancing cheek to cheek to "All I Could Do Was Cry".

Funny. I was thinking exactly the same thing myself ...

Barrington Stoke would like to thank all its readers for commenting on the manuscript before publication and in particular:

Sophie Anscombe
Robyn Atkins
Jessica Burgham
Ann Carr
Judy Carter-Brown
Gemma Clarkson
Amy Greenaway
Joanna Kitson
Mandy Lincoln
Lyuba Lukyanova
Hayley Ross
A. Upton
Tracy Ward

Become a Consultant!

Would you like to give us feedback on our titles before they are published? Contact us at the email address below – we'd love to hear from you!

info@barringtonstoke.co.uk
www.barringtonstoke.co.uk